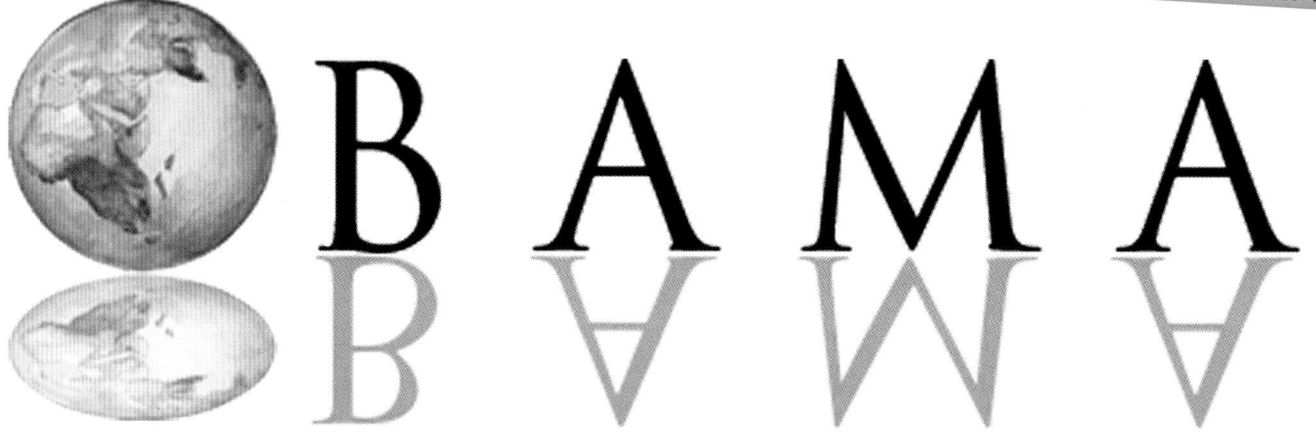

OBAMA

The Day the World Danced

A family heirloom

JAN SPIVEY GILCHRIST

GRAPHIC DESIGN BY: WILLIAM KELVIN GILCHRIST

Everywhere

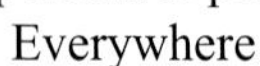

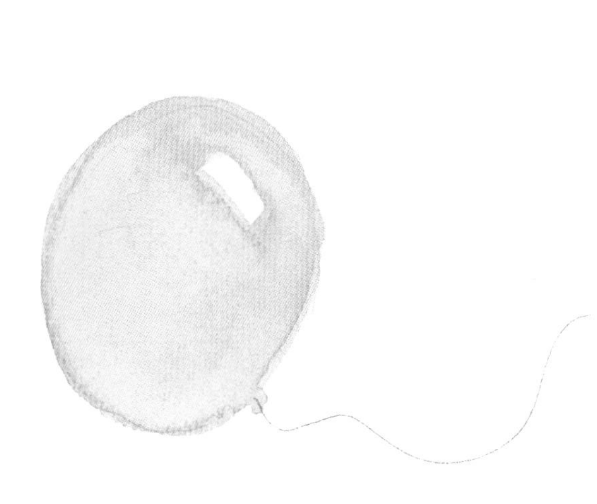

For information address Pegasus Books for Children, P. O. Box 681, Flossmoor, Illinois 60422

Printed in United States
ISBN 978-0-9824095-0-3
First Edition
10 9 8 7 6 5 4 3 2 1

LIBRARY OF CONGRESS CATALOG-IN-PUBLICATION DATA

Jan Spivey Gilchrist

Obama: The Day The World Danced / by Jan Spivey Gilchrist

Summary: Two girls have a sleepover on the night of November 4, 2008 to await the announcement of the 44th President of the United States of America.

For the children of the world,

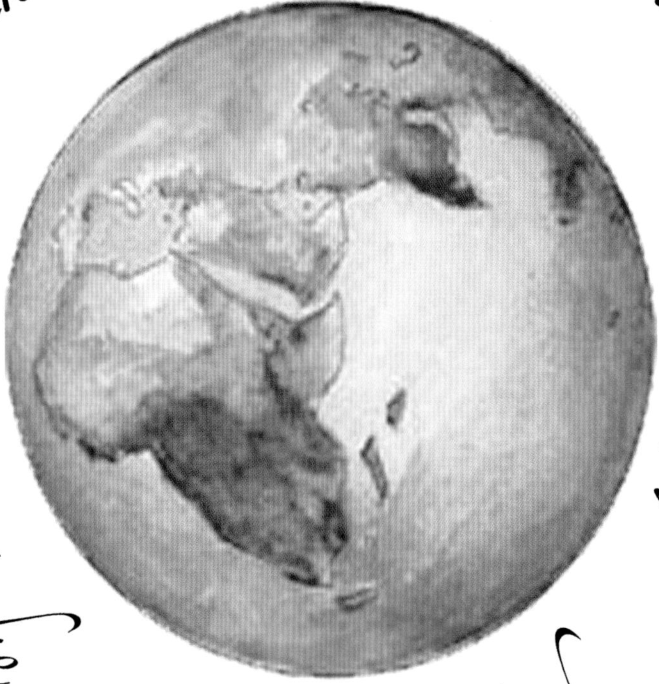

Make a circle around the world

You are making history everyday
keep talking,
keep listening,
keep understanding
keep dancing

J.S.G

They stayed up late.

They wanted to know.

They wanted to see when the world

got the news.

If the world got the news?

Could it really be?

Could it really happen?

Breyna and Emily wanted to watch

him make his speech in their city.

That would be a historic moment.

And they wanted to be right there.

They made memories.

Grandpa popped popcorn that

sounded like tiny crickets dancing,

tap, tap, tap.

Grandma squeezed tangy lemons

that made their noses tingle.

Mama washed sweet juicy grapes

that made their mouths pucker.

And Daddy opened the windows to

let the November summer breeze

fill the rooms of Breyna's house.

They stayed up late. They didn't

want to forget.

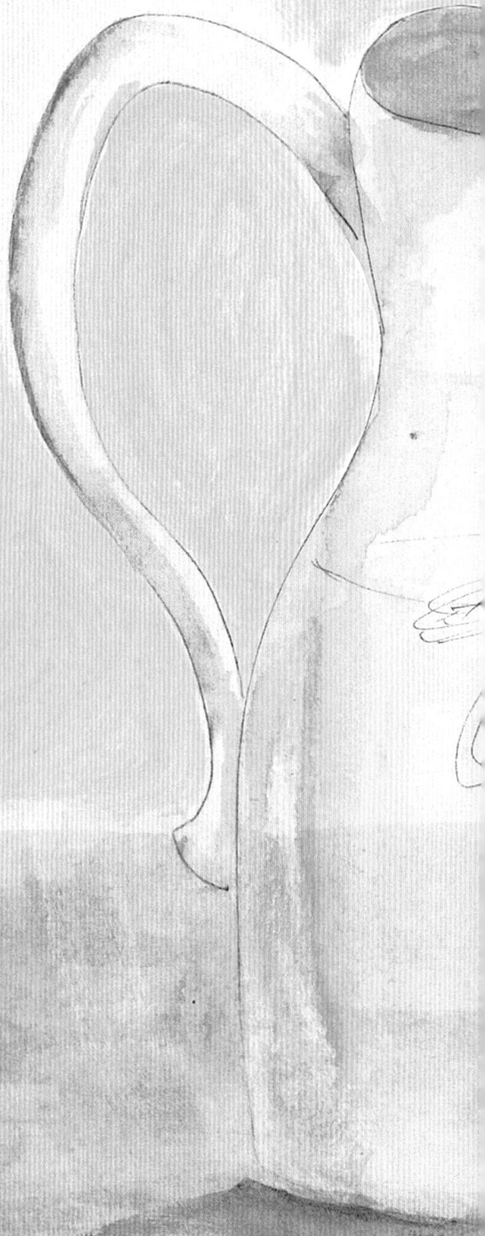

Pop,
pop...pop,
pop,
...pop, pop.

Grandma said, "And just yesterday his grandma Toot said goodbye to him. His Toot followed him as far as she could go. She got him through to his destiny, just like Harriet Tubman, so then she could go home."

"How did she know it was okay to go?" Asked Breyna.

"Grandmas just know, baby." Answered Grandma.

They stayed up late.

They wanted to see history.

They wanted to tell their children about it like their Mamas and Daddies told them.

They wanted to celebrate.

Breyna turned on the TV set.

There were people crowding Grant Park.

The people waved signs. Breyna and Emily read the words on the signs.

They knew those words.

They raced to see who could read them first.

Breyna got pencils, scissors, tape and paper.

"Let's make a book," she said.

"A history book," said Emily, "written and illustrated by Breyna Elizabeth Crude and -"

" And Emily Margaret Frye" interrupted Breyna.

"A family history book like Great Grandma's Bible," yelled Breyna.

"An heirloom," whispered Mama from the kitchen.

"I won't have history," said Emily, "I won't have an heirloom for my family."

"We'll make two. You make yours and I'll make mine," said Breyna.

"That's a great idea," said Emily, "a family heirloom like my great grandfather's watch."

Breyna felt it first, like a stampede of horses in a movie.

Stamping feet, clapping hands.

Waiting, waiting, waiting

and then a loud voice on the television...

"Barack Obama, is the 44th President of the United States!"

"Yeaaaaaaaaaaaaaaaaaaaaaaah!"

Mama and Grandma and Daddy and Grandpa

leaping into the air

yelling,

"Obama, Obama, Yes We Can! Yes We Can!"

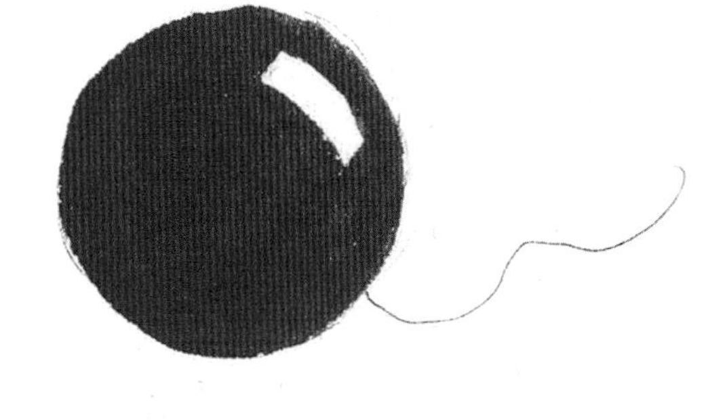

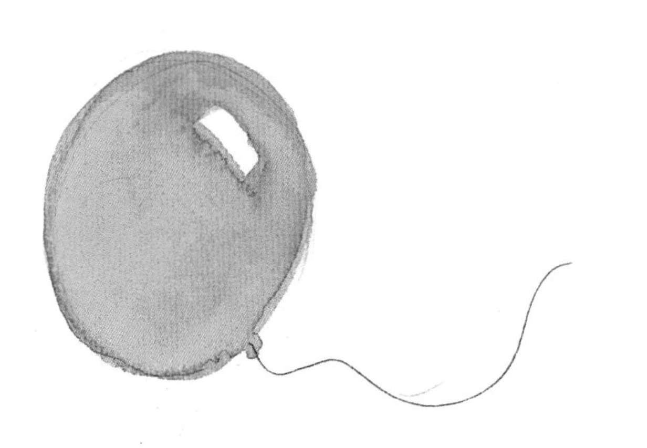

The floor was trembling;

the breeze was blowing.

Breyna's knees shook and her heart beat fast.

She opened her arms,

stretched wide her hands and

reached for Emily.

They pretended to make a circle.

A circle with all the children around the world.

They spun around and then they danced.

Yes, danced. And the people on the TV danced.

The children on the TV danced too.

The children in his father's village in Kenya,

"Obama!"

The children in his old school in Indonesia.

"Obama!"

The children in Hawaii where he lived with his "Toot".

The children in Kansas where his mother was born.

The children in China.

"Obama!"

The children in England.
Obama!

The children in France.

"Obama!"

The children around the world!

A name with music.
A name for change.
A name for hope.
A name for everyone.

"Obama!"

They stayed up late and witnessed history. Then Breyna and Emily knew why the big people were crying, because tears were running down their faces, too.

You have to cry when you see history.

Everyone heard it around the world.

Everyone danced around the world.

And to think that he came from so many places.

But that day Chicago had the sunshine.

Chicago had the November summer.

That night the flag waved in Breyna and Emily’s city,

for their neighbor, their friend, and their Senator.

The flag waved for

Barack Obama,

the

First African American President
of the United States of America.

Create your heirloom

What were you doing on November 4, 2008?